One UFO to Go

Nancy listened carefully. Suddenly she heard a loud creaking sound.

"The garage door is opening," Katie said.

Nancy froze. She gripped her ice-cream cone so hard it almost cracked.

"W-w-what's happening?" Bess stammered.

The door lifted and a powerful beam of light shot out. Nancy covered her eyes with one hand. Bess, George, and Katie did the same.

"It's the spaceship!" Katie screamed. "Don't let the aliens take us!"

The Nancy Drew Notebooks

THE
NANCY DREW
NOTEBOOKS

#23

Alien in the Classroom

CAROLYN KEENE
ILLUSTRATED BY ANTHONY ACCARDO

Aladdin Paperbacks
New York   London   Toronto   Sydney   Singapore

First Aladdin Paperbacks edition May 2002
First Minstrel Books edition March 1998
Copyright © 2004 by Simon & Schuster, Inc

ALADDIN PAPERBACKS
An imprint of Simon & Schuster
Children's Publishing Division
1230 Avenue of the Americas
New York, NY 10020

The text of this book was set in Excelsior.

Manufactured in the United States of America.
20 19 18 17 16 15

ISBN-13: 978-0-671-00818-5
ISBN-10: 0-671-00818-8
0116 OFF

1

Calling All Space Queens!

Is anybody tired yet?" Katie Zaleski asked. It was Saturday night. Katie was having a sleepover party.

Eight-year-old Nancy Drew shook her head. "No way!" she said.

Nancy loved sleepovers. She loved it especially when her two best friends, George Fayne and Bess Marvin, were there.

"I'm glad you're not tired," Katie said. "We're going to stay up all night, no matter how tired we get. Right?"

Nancy glanced at the clock on Katie's night table. It was already nine o'clock. "I've never stayed up all night before," Nancy said.

"If we're going to stay up the whole night," George said, "what are we going to do until morning?"

"Let's try on Mrs. Zaleski's makeup," Bess said. She twirled the ribbon on her pink nightgown. "We can pretend we're supermodels."

"Yuck!" George groaned.

Bess loved pretty clothes. Her cousin George was just the opposite. George preferred flannel pajamas and bare feet to frilly nightgowns and fuzzy bunny slippers.

Lester, Katie's parrot, bobbed his colorful head up and down. "Yuck, yuck, yuck. Squaawwwk!" he said from the top of Katie's bookshelf.

Katie had taught Lester to talk. Now he repeated whatever he heard.

"Hi, boy," Nancy called up to Lester. "Do you want to sing a song?"

Lester walked sideways on the shelf. "Sing, sing, sing!" he cackled.

Katie shook her head. "The only thing Lester will be singing is a lullaby. It's almost his bedtime."

"Bummer!" Lester screeched.

Bess wiggled her fuzzy slippers in the air. "If we can't sing with Lester, what should we do instead?"

"I know," George said. "Let's call snooty Brenda Carlton and hang up."

"I have a better idea," Katie said.

"What?" Nancy asked.

Katie's eyes gleamed. "I'll tell you. But first we have to sit in a circle on the floor."

Bess grabbed a big stuffed bear from Katie's bed. "No scary stories," she said. "Please!"

Nancy, Bess, and George sat cross-legged on the blue-and-white rug. Katie wiggled between George and Bess. She had a newspaper in her hand.

"What is that?" Nancy asked.

"It's the *National Snooper*," Katie said.

"I've seen that in the supermarket. It's usually at the checkout counter, right next to the bubble gum and candy," George said.

"I was about to put it in Lester's cage

3

this morning," Katie said. "That's when I read the front page."

Nancy stared at the headline. She read it out loud: " 'Queen of Planet Zagon to Visit Earth!' "

George's dark eyes opened wide. "A space alien?" she said. "That's cool!"

"I thought you weren't going to tell scary stories!" Bess cried. She covered her face with the stuffed bear.

Katie flipped open the *National Snooper*. There was a picture of an alien with a very large head. The alien was wearing a jeweled crown. Her eyes were like huge black pools. Her green fingers were long and stringy.

"Read it out loud, Katie," George said. "And don't skip a single word."

George leaned over Katie's shoulder. Nancy sat up on her heels. Bess peeked out from behind the bear.

Katie began to read. " 'The queen of planet Zagon is expected to be on her way to Earth at the present time—' "

"You mean right now?" Bess gulped.

Katie went on. " 'The queen may look

and act like an Earthling, but don't let that fool you. She has many powers.' "

"That probably means she has X-ray vision," George said. "She could also have eyes in the back of her head—like the aliens in the movies."

"Peekaboo!" Lester screeched.

"I think this story is made-up," Nancy said with grin.

"You mean you don't believe it?" Katie asked.

"It's an interesting story," Nancy said. "There's no proof that it's true, though."

"No wonder you're a detective, Nancy," Katie said with a laugh.

Nancy was the best detective at Carl Sandburg Elementary School. She had a blue notebook in which she wrote all her clues.

George sat down on Katie's bed. "I hope the story is true. I would love to meet a real-life space alien."

"Even if she has a huge head, green skin, and stringy fingers?" Bess asked.

George nodded, then grinned. "Those are the best kind!"

Katie put the newspaper back on her desk. "I think the queen of planet Zagon could turn up anywhere. She could even be here in River Heights."

"Queen of Zagon! Queen of Zagon!" Lester called out. "ARRRK!"

Katie reached for her pet. "We may be staying up all night, Lester, but you're going back to your cage."

"Nighty-night! Nighty-night!" Lester squawked as Katie carried him to the den.

Nancy and her friends spent the next hour dancing to CDs. Then they played a few of Katie's board games. Then they went to the kitchen to get some ice cream. After watching half of a movie, George pointed to the clock.

"It's after midnight," she said, brushing her dark curls out of her eyes.

"Way after," Bess said, and yawned.

Nancy was tired, too. She began to unroll her sleeping bag. "Maybe we'll stay up all night next time."

Katie turned off the VCR. "Good idea," she said.

The girls lined up their sleeping bags under the window. Nancy loved to look up at the stars before falling asleep.

"The sky looks pretty tonight," Nancy said, snuggling into her sleeping bag.

Bess was already fast asleep.

Katie stared out the window. "Just think. Somewhere up there is planet Zagon."

"And aliens," George said. "Lots and lots of aliens."

Suddenly a bright streak shot across the sky. It left a blazing trail of light.

"Whoa!" George gasped, then sat up in her sleeping bag. "What was that?"

Nancy looked out the window. "It's the biggest shooting star I've ever seen."

"That's not a star," Katie whispered. "It's the queen of planet Zagon traveling down to Earth!"

*   *   *

On Monday morning Nancy, Bess, George, and Katie walked together to Mrs. Reynolds's third-grade class.

Katie reached into her backpack. "Guess what? I brought in the article about the queen of planet Zagon."

Bess wrinkled her nose. "Why?"

"For current events," Katie said.

Nancy followed her friends into Mrs. Reynolds's classroom. Their teacher was not there, though. Instead, a woman with shiny black hair and a bright smile greeted them at the door.

Who's she? Nancy wondered. And where is Mrs. Reynolds?

All the students took their seats. Nancy sat in the third row next to Bess. Katie's desk was right behind Nancy's. George sat farther back.

"Good morning, boys and girls," the woman announced. "Mrs. Reynolds has a bad cold so she'll be absent all week."

Whispers filled the classroom. Mike Minelli raised his hand. "Who are you?" he asked.

"I'm your substitute teacher," the

9

woman explained. "And my name is . . ."

She turned to the board and began to write.

Nancy whispered as the letters appeared one by one. "Ms. Z-A-G . . ."

"Ms. Zigzag?" Bess giggled softly.

"Z-A-G-O-N," Nancy read.

Suddenly Nancy's blue eyes opened wide. "Ms. *Zagon?*"

2

Prove It . . . Or Else!

"Oh, no!" Bess whispered to Nancy. "Our substitute teacher is the queen of planet Zagon!"

Nancy turned around in her seat to look at George.

"The queen of planet Zagon?" Katie gasped. "In our class? Eek!"

Ms. Zagon looked up from her desk. "Is anything wrong?" she asked Katie.

"N-no, Ms. Zagon," Katie said. "I just have the, uh, hiccups." Then she made the sound. "Hic, hic, hic!"

Brenda Carlton turned around. "Stand on your head and drink a glass of water," she said. She looked at her

11

best friend, Alison Wegman, and giggled.

Ms. Zagon held up a pile of colorful papers and some black markers. "I'd like you all to make name tags for your desks," she said. "I'll know your names by the end of the day."

While Ms. Zagon passed out the supplies, Nancy and her friends leaned across the aisle and whispered.

"She *is* the queen of planet Zagon," Katie said. "I just know it."

"Why else would her name be Ms. Zagon?" Bess added.

"She can't be from outer space," Nancy said. "Ms. Zagon seems nice."

"So was E.T.," Bess murmured.

After all the kids had finished their name tags, Ms. Zagon walked to the board. "Mrs. Reynolds left a list of new spelling words she wanted you to learn," she said.

Nancy watched Ms. Zagon write ten new words on the board.

Ms. Zagon is just an ordinary teacher, Nancy thought as she copied

down the words. She's just like Mrs. Reynolds.

After spelling, the class did some math problems. Soon it was time for lunch.

"Now we can talk more about Ms. Zagon," Katie said as the four friends walked into the lunchroom. They sat down at their favorite table by the window.

"I like Ms. Zagon," Nancy said, pulling a peanut butter sandwich from her lunch box.

Katie smiled. "Don't you see? That's her trick, Nancy. She wants us to like her, so it'll be easy to take over our planet."

George glanced from side to side. Then she whispered, "What we know about Ms. Zagon should be our secret. Don't tell anyone, especially Brenda."

Bess nodded as she opened her flowered lunch box. "And don't tell any boys."

"I wonder where Ms. Zagon keeps her spaceship," Katie said.

"I wonder why Ms. Zagon doesn't have antennas?" George asked.

"She probably keeps them hidden under her high hairdo," Bess answered.

"I once saw a movie where an alien made all the animals on Earth grow bigger and bigger," George said. She spread her arms wide as she spoke.

"Even the worms got bigger?" Bess asked.

Nancy smiled. Bess really hated worms. "Don't worry, Bess," Nancy said, taking a bite of her sandwich. "Ms. Zagon isn't an alien."

"Who's not an alien?"

The girls looked up to see Brenda Carlton.

"I said, who's not an alien?" Brenda repeated, taking a seat next to Nancy.

"Nobody's an alien," Nancy insisted.

"If *you* won't tell me, Nancy," Brenda said, clunking down a container of strawberry yogurt, "I know who will."

Brenda leaned over the table and stared at Bess. "Guess what, Bess?" she asked sweetly. "I'm writing a new article on your favorite subject—worms!"

"W-w-worms?" Bess gulped. "Eeeww!"

Uh-oh, Nancy thought. Brenda's trying to *worm* the information out of Bess.

"Quit it, Brenda," George ordered.

Brenda went on. "I'm writing about all kinds of worms. Fat worms, skinny worms—"

George put her hands over Bess's ears, but it was no use.

"Even worms that wiggle in and out of tuna fish sandwiches!" Brenda shouted.

Bess dropped her tuna fish sandwich on the table. "Stop it!" she begged.

"I'll stop—as soon as you tell me who the alien is," Brenda said. Then she began to sing. "The worms crawl in, the worms crawl out—"

"Our substitute teacher is the queen of planet Zagon!" Bess blurted out.

Brenda's mouth dropped open. "Ms. Zagon is from another planet?"

"No, she's not," Nancy said.

16

"Yes, she is," Katie insisted. Then she told Brenda everything.

"There goes our secret," George mumbled as she peeled a banana.

"Wow!" Brenda said. "A real-life space alien right here at Carl Sandburg. What a great story for the *Carlton News*."

The *Carlton News* was the newspaper that Brenda wrote at home.

"Brenda, you can't write a story about Ms. Zagon," Nancy said.

"This story is too hot *not* to write, Nancy," Brenda said, sticking out her chin.

"But it's probably not true!" Nancy cried.

"Then *prove* it's not true," Brenda snapped. "If you prove that Ms. Zagon isn't an alien, I won't write the story."

"Don't do it, Nancy," George whispered.

Brenda went on. "You *are* the school's best detective, aren't you?"

Nancy took a sip of milk. She didn't want to prove anything to Brenda. But she didn't want her writing lies about Ms. Zagon, either.

"Okay, I'll do it," Nancy said. "And it will be a cinch."

Brenda dipped her spoon into her yogurt. "Good. Because you have two days to prove that Ms. Zagon isn't an alien. That's when my next issue will come out."

Katie counted on her fingers. "That's by Wednesday!"

Nancy looked Brenda right in the eye. "And what if I don't?" she asked.

"Then I print the story," Brenda said, getting up from her chair. "On the front page."

The bell rang. Nancy, Bess, George, and Katie finished their lunch and walked together to their classroom.

"Maybe Ms. Zagon will take Brenda back to her planet," Katie told Bess and Nancy as they took their seats.

Bess and Nancy giggled. "That would be awesome!" Bess said.

Ms. Zagon walked to the front of the

classroom. "Did you all have a nice lunch?" she asked the class.

"Yes, Ms. Zagon!" the kids replied.

"Good," Ms. Zagon said. "Because now we're going to study my favorite subject. She reached under her desk and pulled up a huge, colorful map of the nine planets.

"Let's talk about outer space!"

3

Take Me to Your Leader

Outer space?" Katie whispered over Nancy's shoulder. "Didn't I tell you?"

There has to be a reason, Nancy thought. There has to be!

"I love the planets so much," Ms. Zagon said, gazing at the map. "And I like to consider myself an expert on space travel."

Brenda turned around and grinned at Nancy. "I told you so," she whispered.

Mike Minelli called out without raising his hand. "I'm an expert, too, Ms. Zagon. My friends and I watch *Moleheads from Mars* on TV every Saturday."

"You're an expert because you and

your friends are all space cadets," Brenda said. Everyone laughed.

Ms. Zagon just smiled, then she began the lesson. "Mercury is a very hot planet," she began. She pointed to the planets one by one. "And Pluto is a very cold planet," she said at the end.

Then she explained how all of the planets moved around the sun.

"How come they don't bump into each other?" Andrew Leoni asked.

"That's a very good question, Andrew," Ms. Zagon said. "The reason is that they're millions of miles apart."

Wow, Nancy thought.

Ms. Zagon turned back to the board. She wrote down the names of the planets.

"Jupiter . . . Saturn . . ."

Nancy glanced across the classroom. She saw Jason crunching a spitball in his fist. He had a mean look on his face.

"Jason Hutchings," Ms. Zagon called out as she wrote. "Please don't throw that spitball."

Jason looked surprised as he dropped the spitball on his desk.

How did Ms. Zagon know that Jason was about to throw a spitball when she was facing the board? Nancy wondered. Unless she has eyes in back of her head—just like an alien!

Ms. Zagon faced the class. "Phoebe Archer? Please take the candy bar out of your pocket and put it in your lunch box."

"Okay." Phoebe sighed. She pulled a half-eaten Panda Crunch bar from her shirt pocket.

How did Ms. Zagon know that Phoebe had a candy bar in her pocket? Nancy wondered. Unless she has X-ray vision—just like an alien!

Nancy shook her head. There must be an explanation for all this, she thought.

The afternoon went quickly. When the bell rang at three o'clock, Ms. Zagon smiled at the class. "I'll see you all tomorrow. Class dismissed."

"Did you see the way she looked at

that map?" Bess said when they were outside. "It's as if she was homesick."

Katie grabbed Nancy's arm. She pointed toward the street. "Look. There she is!"

Nancy saw Ms. Zagon stepping into a bright red car with a black top. "See?" Nancy said. "Ms. Zagon doesn't drive a spaceship. She drives an ordinary car with four wheels."

Katie gasped as Ms. Zagon began to drive away. "But look at her license plate."

George read it aloud. "It says, 2 EARTH."

"How do you explain that, Detective Drew?" Katie asked, folding her arms across her chest.

"Yeah," Bess said. "And how are you going to solve this mystery?"

Nancy knew she would have to work fast. "Let's meet at the Double Dip at four," she suggested. "I always think better over ice cream."

The four girls ran home to get permission to ride their bikes to Main

Street. Twenty minutes later they parked their bicycles in front of the Double Dip, their favorite ice-cream parlor.

After getting their cones, they sat around a small wooden table. Nancy held a chocolate mint ice-cream cone in one hand, and a pencil in the other. Her notebook with the shiny blue cover was opened to a fresh page.

Katie, Bess, and George watched as Nancy wrote "The Alien Mystery" at the top of the page.

"I'll start by making a list of all the reasons Ms. Zagon can't be an alien," Nancy said.

"What if you find clues that Ms. Zagon *is* an alien?" Katie asked.

Nancy tapped her pencil against the table. Then her eyes lit up. "I know!"

She drew a line down the page. At the top of one column she wrote "Alien." At the top of the other she wrote "Human."

"What are you doing?" Katie asked.

"I'm going to make a checklist," Nancy explained.

"You think of everything, Nancy," George said.

Nancy licked her ice-cream cone and thought for a moment. "I wish I could find out where Ms. Zagon lives. Then I could prove that she lives in a house and not in a spaceship."

George shook her dark curls. "Aliens don't live in their spaceship when they come to Earth. They park it somewhere until they're ready to return to their planet."

Bess shivered. "That's creepy!"

Katie pointed to Nancy's notebook. "Write on your Alien list that Ms. Zagon has eyes in the back of her head."

"And X-ray vision," George added.

Nancy wrote the words in her notebook. "I'm also going to write that Ms. Zagon is nice and drives a car. I'll put that on the Human side."

"But she's got weird license plates," George said.

Nancy added that information to the Alien side.

Just then Katie shrieked. "Look out the window, everyone. Quick!"

Two figures in shiny silver space suits were walking by. Their heads were large and pointed at the top.

"They look like visitors from another planet!" George gasped.

They sure do, Nancy thought.

"I'll bet they're headed for Ms. Zagon's spaceship," Katie said. "We have to follow them."

"But what if they see us?" Bess asked.

"We'll offer them our ice-cream cones," George suggested.

Nancy wasn't sure if the creatures were really aliens. But she knew there was only one way to find out.

"Okay, let's follow them," she said.

The girls took their cones outside and began to walk down the street.

"We have to stick close together," Nancy said firmly. Then she stopped. Bess bumped into Nancy.

"Not *that* close," Nancy said.

Katie pulled Nancy's arm. "The aliens are turning the corner. Let's hurry!"

Still holding their ice-cream cones, the girls marched down Main Street. When they reached the corner, they slowed down.

"They're going into that yellow house with the green shutters," Katie whispered.

The four girls watched the creatures walk through the door. Their silver space suits glowed brightly in the late afternoon sun.

When the creatures were inside the house, the girls tiptoed quietly up the driveway.

"Wait," Nancy whispered. "I think I hear a noise."

"What is it?" George whispered.

Nancy listened carefully. Suddenly she heard a loud creaking sound.

"The garage door is opening," Katie said, stepping back.

Nancy froze. She gripped her ice-cream cone so hard it almost cracked.

"W-w-what's happening?" Bess stammered.

The door lifted and a powerful beam of light shot out. Nancy covered her eyes with one hand. Bess, George, and Katie did the same.

"It's the spaceship!" Katie screamed. "Don't let the aliens take us!"

4

2 Earth 2 Soon

Leave us alone!" Nancy shouted toward the blinding light.

"Yeah!" George yelled. "Pick on someone from your own planet!"

The light began to fade. Nancy uncovered her eyes. But instead of looking straight at space aliens, she was staring at—

"The boys!" Bess groaned.

Mike, Jason, David Berger, and two other boys were standing inside the garage, wearing the silver space suits. They held blue plastic space guns. David was holding a large, high-beam flashlight.

David stepped forward. "We caught

you spying on our new club," he said in a fake alien voice. "This means war!"

"Club?" Nancy asked. "What club?"

"Our *Moleheads from Mars* fan club," Mike said proudly.

Jason pumped his fist in the air. "Moleheads rule!" he shouted.

"Give me a break," George said.

David tilted his head. "You thought we were *real* aliens, didn't you?" he asked.

Nancy made herself laugh loudly. "Real aliens? You? No way."

A boy with red hair and freckles scowled at the girls. "Did so. I saw you and you were scared."

Katie made a face. "Why would we be scared by you when we happen to know a real-life alien right here in River Heights?"

"A real alien?" Mike cried.

"Who? Where?" Jason demanded.

Bess stuck out her chin. "We're not telling. It's a secret!"

David raised his plastic space gun. "Tell us everything or we'll fire."

"There are no aliens in River Heights," Nancy said.

George pointed to the boys. "Just a bunch of jerks in aluminum foil suits."

The girls giggled as they licked their melting ice-cream cones.

Then a boy with blond hair and glasses raised his space gun. "Attack!" he shouted.

Nancy and her friends screamed as sticky string spurted from the boys' plastic space guns. The colorful string tangled in their hair and around their arms and legs.

"Gross!" Nancy yelled as the sticky string whipped around her ice-cream cone.

"Creeps!" Katie shouted.

The boys just laughed.

"Let's get out of here," Nancy said to her friends.

As the girls walked away from the house, Nancy heard Jason shout something at them.

"If there's an alien in River Heights,

we're going to catch it, not you!" he called.

"I don't know what's worse," Nancy said as they hurried back to Main Street. "Finding aliens or those boys."

"Moleheads." George laughed. She pulled a piece of yellow string from one of her curls. "Meatheads is more like it."

"I don't think I'll ever eat strawberry fudge ripple ever again," Bess said, wiping ice cream from her face.

As the girls walked over to their bikes, Nancy spotted Ms. Zagon's red car parked a few feet away. It had the strange license plate that read 2 EARTH.

"There's Ms. Zagon's car," Nancy said. "I want to look inside."

"Why?" George asked.

"Because I still want to prove that Ms. Zagon drives a normal car, that's why," Nancy explained.

Nancy, George, Katie, and Bess surrounded the car. They pressed their noses against the windows.

"Just as I thought!" Katie cried.

"What is it?" Nancy asked.

"Ms. Zagon has a bag of marshmallows on her backseat," Katie answered.

Nancy stared at Katie. "What's wrong with marshmallows?" she asked.

"Marshmallow has the word *Mars* in it," Katie said. "Maybe it's not a bag of marshmallows but a secret alien potion to put us under her power."

"Katie, I think you're getting carried away," Nancy said with a laugh.

"This car looks okay to me," Bess said.

"You see?" Nancy said, looking through the window again. "Ms. Zagon drives an ordinary car just like—"

Nancy stopped talking when she saw it. On the front seat was a picture of four saucer-eyed aliens with huge heads and stringy fingers. Over one of the aliens was an arrow and the word *me.*

"Check it out," Nancy said, pointing to the picture.

"If those aren't aliens," Katie said, "I'll eat Lester's birdseed!"

"But Ms. Zagon doesn't look like that," Bess said. "Those creatures have green skin."

Katie jammed her finger against the window. "That's what she *really* looks like—when she doesn't have her Earth makeup on."

Nancy looked at the picture. Could Ms. Zagon be an alien after all? she wondered.

Suddenly Nancy felt as though someone was watching her. She held her breath and turned around very slowly.

Then Nancy saw her.

"Hello, girls."

Nancy felt her heart pound in her chest.

Standing in front of her was Ms. Zagon!

5

Lester the Spy

I see you found my car," Ms. Zagon said with a smile. "Want a marshmallow?"

The girls didn't answer. They ran to their bikes and rode off, screaming all the way home.

Before dinner Nancy sat on her bed. She opened her blue notebook and wrote "weird picture" on her Alien list.

"Phooey!" Nancy said to herself. "The Alien list is much longer than the Human list."

"Nancy! Dinner!" Hannah Gruen called from the dining room. Hannah was the Drews' housekeeper.

Nancy shut her notebook and hurried

downstairs. She sat down at the table and stared at her plate.

"The macaroni," Nancy said slowly. "It's shaped like flying saucers."

"Yes," Hannah said. "I saw it at the supermarket and thought it was cute."

Nancy put down her fork and sighed.

"Aren't you hungry, Pudding Pie?" Carson Drew asked.

"Yes, Daddy," Nancy said. "But first I have a question."

Carson winked. "Shoot."

"What if you're trying to prove that you're right, and you start finding out that you might be wrong?"

Carson took a sip of water. "There's nothing wrong with being wrong. As long as you can admit it."

Nancy thought for a moment. "I'm not wrong yet. But I feel as if I'm not getting anywhere with my new mystery."

"Don't give up, Pudding Pie," Carson said. "You might be a lot closer than you think."

Nancy smiled and ate a forkful of

macaroni. It tasted good—for flying saucers.

I have one more day to solve this case, Nancy told herself after dinner. Then she thought about how she could prove that Ms. Zagon was not an alien. If only I could find out where she lives, she thought.

With her puppy, Chocolate Chip, at her heels, Nancy went into the den. She dragged the heavy phone book from her father's desk and opened it to the Z's.

" 'Zafowitz . . . Zager . . . Zagon,' " Nancy read out loud. " 'Diana Lynn Zagon.' That must be her."

She wrote Ms. Zagon's name, telephone number, and address under the Human column in her notebook.

Nancy smiled down at her dog. "Now we're getting somewhere, Chip."

On Tuesday morning Nancy and her friends headed to their classroom.

"Are you sure the name in the phone book was Ms. Zagon's?" George asked Nancy.

"I'm almost positive," Nancy said firmly. She looked at Katie. "And aliens are *not* listed in the phone book."

Katie put her hands on her hips. "I'll bet aliens can make their names appear in the phone book if they want to."

"Aliens can do anything," Bess said.

"That does it," Nancy said. "We're all going to go to Ms. Zagon's address right after school. Then we can see her house."

"I wish we could find out what's going on *inside* her house," George said.

"Good idea," Nancy said. "Maybe we'll be able to."

"But how?" Katie asked. "And what if Ms. Zagon catches us?"

"Yeah," Bess said. "What if Ms. Zagon catches us?"

Katie rolled her eyes. "I just said that, Bess. You're beginning to sound like Lester."

Nancy snapped her fingers. "That's it. We can use Lester!"

The girls formed a huddle in front of their classroom.

"Lester repeats everything he hears, right?" Nancy whispered.

"Of course," Katie said. "He's a parrot."

"So why don't we fly him into Ms. Zagon's house and then listen to what he says when he comes out?" Nancy asked.

"No way," Katie said. "Lester's not a spy. He's my pet."

George grabbed Katie's shoulders. "And now he can be a hero."

Katie stared at George. "A hero?"

"Sure," George said with a smile. "If Lester winds up saving the whole planet, he'll be more famous than Lassie."

"More famous than Lassie . . ." Katie leaned against the wall and whistled low. "Okay, I'll do it."

Nancy smiled. "Good. We'll make a plan during lunch."

As they walked into the classroom,

Nancy asked, "Are you still coming to my house for dinner?"

George and Bess nodded. They had gotten permission the night before.

"I can't," Katie said. "I'll have to bring Lester right home."

"That's okay," Nancy said. "I'll ask Hannah to save you some dessert."

Once in the classroom Nancy saw a group of kids surrounding the hamster cage.

"What's going on?" Nancy asked Emily Reeves.

Emily pointed to one of the class hamsters. "Look at Peaches. All of a sudden she's so big and fat."

Nancy stared at the chubby hamster. She remembered the movie in which the alien made animals grow bigger and bigger.

"Add that to your Alien list, Nancy," Katie whispered.

Ms. Zagon spent the day teaching math, social studies, and talking about more planets. After school the girls picked up Lester. Then they walked to Ms. Zagon's house.

"What time is it?" George asked.

"It's three forty-five," Nancy said, looking at her purple watch.

Katie held Lester's cage tightly. "Let's get this over with," she said nervously.

"Over with! Over with!" Lester squawked.

"For a spy, he's sure got a big mouth," Bess complained.

The girls tiptoed across the lawn and right up to the house. They peeked through one of the windows.

"I see Ms. Zagon," Nancy whispered. "She's talking on the telephone."

"She's probably reporting to her leader," Katie whispered.

Nancy and her friends gathered behind a clump of bushes and went over their plans.

"First, we'll let Lester fly through an open window. After about ten minutes we'll ring Ms. Zagon's bell."

George continued. "Then we'll ask Ms. Zagon if she found a lost parrot."

"After we get Lester back," Katie went on, "we'll listen to what he says."

The girls found an open window on the side of the house.

"Slip Lester inside the house here," Nancy told Katie.

Katie lifted Lester out of his cage and placed him on the window ledge. Then she gently pushed him inside the house.

"AAAARK!" Lester squawked.

Nancy watched through the window.

"He's making his way through the house," Nancy said, giving the thumbs-up sign. "Now all we have to do is wait."

The girls sat on the ground under the window. After a few minutes Nancy heard a loud fluttering sound above her head. She stood up and saw Lester flapping his wings against the window.

"Lester's back!" Nancy cried.

"He looks scared," Bess said.

Katie reached into the window and

helped her pet out of the house. "You'd be scared too if you came face-to-face with an alien."

"Lester," Nancy said. "What's new?"

Lester stared at Nancy and blinked.

"He's not talking," George said, concerned.

Katie shook her parrot gently. "Lester. Say something. Anything!"

Lester stretched his neck. Then he opened his beak wide.

"VEEGATESDEERGROSSMUDDER!" he screeched.

"What did he say?" Nancy asked.

"VEEGATESDEERGROSSMUDDER!"

"What a strange word!" Bess said.

Katie looked as if she was about to cry. "What did Ms. Zagon do to my parrot?"

"Don't worry," Nancy said. "He's probably just repeating what Ms. Zagon said on the phone."

"If that's true," Katie said, her green eyes flashing, "then Lester is speaking the secret language of planet Zagon!"

6

X Marks the Spot

It can't be a secret language," Nancy insisted.

"What else could it be?" George asked. "Lester only repeats what he hears."

Lester stretched his neck. "VEE-GATESDEERGROSSMUDDER!"

"Write that down in your notebook, Nancy," Katie said.

"Write it?" Nancy cried. "I can't even say it!"

"I don't like this," Bess said, her voice sounding shaky.

Katie rested her cheek on Lester's feathers. "Lester will never be the same again. I've lost him forever."

Nancy noticed a rolled-up paper in Lester's claw. "What could that be?" she asked.

"Oh, Lester is always grabbing things." Katie sighed. "Once he flew off with my homework."

Nancy tried to tug the paper from Lester's claw, but he wouldn't let go.

"See?" Katie said. "He's even acting strange."

"Please give it to me, Lester," Nancy begged.

Lester pulled his claw away from Nancy. "VEEGATESDEERGROSSMUD-DER!" he squawked.

"Try tickling him," Katie suggested.

Nancy made a face. She carefully tickled Lester's feathery chest with her finger. "Kitchy, kitchy, koo."

"Hee, hee, hee, hee!" Lester cackled. He dropped the paper, and Nancy snatched it up.

"Got it!" Nancy said happily.

"Is anybody out there?" a voice called from inside the house.

"It's Ms. Zagon," Bess whispered.

Nancy stuffed the paper into her pocket. Katie pushed Lester back into his cage.

"VEEGATESDEER—"

"Shh," Nancy warned.

The girls leaned against the side of the house. When the coast was clear, they hurried back to the sidewalk and ran all the way to Main Street.

When they were a safe distance away, Nancy pulled the mysterious paper from her pocket. She began to unroll it.

"That was the scariest thing we've ever done," Bess said.

"Speaking of scary," George said. "Look who's coming."

Brenda Carlton was walking up the street with her mother. When Mrs. Carlton stopped to look at a store window, Brenda walked over.

Nancy hid the paper behind her back. "Hi, Brenda," she said quickly.

Brenda looked at Lester. "What's Cracker Breath doing here?"

Lester pecked at his cage.

"We just came from the grocery store," Katie said. "Lester likes to pick out his own crackers."

Nancy giggled.

Brenda looked at Nancy. "Have you proved that Ms. Zagon isn't an alien yet?"

Nancy squeezed the paper behind her back. "I still have until tomorrow, remember?" she answered.

"Good luck," Brenda said. "Because I've already started writing the article."

"Snooty pants," Katie whispered as Brenda walked back to her mother.

Just then Lester opened his mouth and screeched loudly, "Snooty pants! Snooty pants! ARRRK!"

Brenda spun around angrily. She stuck her tongue out at the girls, then ran to catch up with her mother.

"Lester is cured!" Katie let out a big sigh. Nancy, Bess, and George jumped up and down and cheered.

When Brenda and Mrs. Carlton were out of sight, Nancy carefully unrolled the mysterious paper that Lester had taken from Ms. Zagon's house.

"What is it, Nancy?" Katie asked, placing Lester's cage on the sidewalk.

Nancy examined the paper. It had all sorts of squiggly lines and arrows. On top were the words "Carl Sandburg Elementary School."

"It's a map of our school grounds," Nancy said.

"Why would anyone need a map of the school?" Bess said. "It's not that big."

Katie shrugged. "Ms. Zagon probably needs lots of maps to get around Earth. It's like she's on vacation down here."

Nancy followed the little arrows on the map with her finger. They led to a bright red X under the drawing of a tree.

"That's the big oak in back of the school," George said. "I tried to climb it once."

"Wait a minute," Nancy said. "There's something written under the X."

Nancy squinted her eyes to read. "It says 'capsule.' "

"Capsule?" George repeated slowly.

The four girls looked at each other.

"I know what it is!" Katie shouted. "It's a map giving directions to Ms. Zagon's space capsule!"

7

Buried Treasure

Nancy shook her head. "Don't you think we would have seen a space capsule parked behind the school?"

"Maybe it's covered with trees or bushes," Katie suggested.

"We have to go to the school and check it out," George insisted.

Nancy looked at her watch. "It's four-thirty. Hannah said we could stay out until dinner, so we have time."

"Let's go get Chocolate Chip, Nancy," Bess begged. "We might need a dog to protect us."

Katie picked up Lester's cage. "I'm going home. Lester's been scared enough for one day. So have I."

Nancy knew how Katie felt. She wasn't quite sure if she wanted to go herself.

It was almost five o'clock when Nancy, Bess, and George returned to the Drew house.

"Hannah?" Nancy asked. "Can we walk Chip over to the school?"

Chip wagged her tail happily.

Hannah looked puzzled. "Why the school, Nancy?"

"Chip likes the school yard," Nancy said. "There's lots of space over there."

George gulped. "Space?" she repeated.

Nancy nudged George lightly.

"I suppose it's fine. But be back home by a quarter to six," Hannah said. "I just put a pan of lasagna in the oven."

"Lasagna!" Bess cried. "Yum!"

"We promise, Hannah," Nancy said, clipping on Chip's leash.

The girls left the house and walked briskly to the school. When they reached the school yard, they saw some other kids playing on the swings and jumping rope.

"Ugh," Bess said. She made a face. "There's Jason, David, and Mike."

The boys were walking slowly around the playground. They were waving long plastic rods with flashing lights at one end.

"What are they doing?" Bess asked.

"They're using alien detectors," Nancy explained. "I've seen commercials for them on TV."

"Boys and their stupid toys," George said.

"I don't want them to see us," Nancy warned. She grabbed Chip's leash and led her friends to the back of the school.

"I don't see any space capsule around here," George said.

Suddenly a round, flat disk soared over their heads.

"Eeek!" Bess shrieked.

"A flying saucer!" George screamed.

The object landed at Nancy's feet. She laughed. "It's a Frisbee."

A fifth-grade boy ran over. "Throw it back!" he shouted.

Nancy threw the Frisbee to the boy.

"Thanks," the boy called. He caught it and ran back around the school.

Then Chip barked.

"What is it, girl?" Nancy asked.

"Maybe Chip sees an alien," George said.

Nancy pointed to a small, furry animal scurrying by. "It looks more like a field mouse."

Chip tugged at her leash. Nancy strained to pull her back.

"Chip, no!" Nancy commanded.

But it was no use. Chip broke loose from Nancy's grip and began chasing the little animal.

"Chip, come back here!" Nancy called.

The mouse was too fast for Chip. He dashed over to the oak tree, popped into the ground, and disappeared.

Chip barked at the hole and began to dig after the mouse.

"Oh, no," Bess wailed. "That's where the space capsule is supposed to be!"

Chip stopped digging. She lifted her paw and brought it down on something hard. It made a tapping noise.

"Chip's found something!" George exclaimed.

Nancy knelt down and brushed away some loose dirt. "It's a black metal box," she said. The box was rusty and closed with a silver hinge.

Bess sighed with relief. "It looks too small to be a space capsule."

George lifted the box from the ground. "Oof! It's as heavy as a space-ship. Let's open it."

"We should find out what it is first," Nancy said. She tugged at the box in George's arms. "Let's put it back."

"Let's go home!" Bess wailed.

Nancy and George struggled with the box. Chip barked and jumped up on Nancy.

"Oh, no!" Nancy groaned as the box slipped from her arms. It tumbled to the ground and snapped open.

Nancy held her breath as everything inside the box spilled out. No one said a word as they stared down at the ground.

"I'm going to investigate," Nancy finally said. She knelt down and sifted through the things.

"What is it?" Bess asked.

"It's all sorts of stuff," Nancy said. "From Carl Sandburg Elementary School."

Nancy picked up a Carl Sandburg school hat. "Look at the date on the brim," she said. "It's from twenty-five years ago."

"So is this," George said, kneeling down next to Nancy. She held up a Carl Sandburg school pin. "And it says 'Have a Groovy Year!'"

"Let me see," Bess said, inching her way over.

The girls examined more objects. George read an old report card for a boy named Scott. Nancy found a newspaper. On the front page was a president they had learned about in history class.

"These clothes were cool!" Bess said. She held up a fashion magazine showing a model with a splashy flowered dress.

Suddenly Nancy spotted a book with a dark red cover. It was an old school yearbook.

"Why was all this neat stuff buried in a box?" George asked, trying on the hat.

Nancy scratched her chin. "An old yearbook, an old hat, an old report card . . . I know!"

Bess and George stared at Nancy.

"This isn't a space capsule," Nancy said. "It's a *time* capsule."

"A time capsule?" Bess repeated.

Nancy nodded. "A Carl Sandburg class probably buried this stuff over twenty years ago."

George whistled. "Wow!"

"Like this yearbook," Nancy said. She picked it up and opened it to the last page. It was covered with pictures of smiling third graders.

Nancy read the names out loud: " 'Beth Zachar, Anthony Zaffino, Diana Lynn Zagon . . .' " Nancy's mouth dropped open.

"As in *Ms*. Zagon?" George asked.

Nancy pointed to a picture of a girl with long, dark hair. "That must be Ms. Zagon when she was eight years old."

Chip nuzzled the page with her nose.

Bess smiled at the picture. "Ms. Zagon had a hairdo just like mine."

Nancy found a piece of paper inside the yearbook. "Here's a composition called, 'Why I Love Astronomy.' It's written by Diana Lynn Zagon."

Bess chuckled. "Ms. Zagon loved the planets back then, too."

"I can't believe Ms. Zagon went to Carl Sandburg," George said.

"That's it!" Nancy shouted. "This is the proof I need that Ms. Zagon is not an alien!"

"You're right," George said, and gave Nancy a high five.

"If Ms. Zagon went to our school twenty-five years ago, she couldn't be a recent visitor from outer space," Nancy said happily.

"Or the queen of planet Zagon," Bess added.

Nancy touched the black metal box. "This was probably the surprise Ms. Zagon was talking about."

"The school must have given her permission to dig it up," George said.

"Let's call Katie right after dinner," Bess suggested. "I can't wait to tell her the news."

Nancy rubbed her hands together. "And I can't wait to tell Brenda."

"Let's call her, too," George said.

Nancy shook her head. "I'll tell Brenda in school tomorrow. I want to see her face when she finds out that I solved the mystery."

"What are we going to do with all this stuff in the meantime?" George asked.

"Let's put the time capsule back

where we found it," Nancy said. "Then we'd better hurry back to my house."

George rubbed her stomach. "And Hannah's lasagna."

The next morning Nancy went to school feeling great.

"I never *really* thought Ms. Zagon was an alien," Katie told Nancy as they walked into the classroom.

"Yeah, right." Nancy laughed.

Suddenly Bess grabbed Nancy's arm. "Nancy, look!"

Nancy froze. The kids were sitting at their desks busily reading the *Carlton News*. On the front page was Nancy's school picture. The headline underneath the picture read, "Nancy Drew Discovers a Space Alien at Carl Sandburg."

"Oh, no!" Nancy cried.

"Good morning, Nancy," Brenda called sweetly from her desk.

Nancy glared at Brenda. "I had until today to solve the mystery, Brenda!"

Brenda spread her arms wide. "Well, your time is up."

Jason Hutchings looked up from his copy of the *Carlton News*. "Hey, Nancy. Did you really catch Ms. Zagon fueling up her spaceship?"

"No!" Nancy cried.

"And did you really catch Ms. Zagon polishing her antennas?" Phoebe Archer asked.

Nancy's heart sank. Brenda's article was full of lies about her. *Big* lies!

Suddenly the door opened. Ms. Oshida, the assistant principal, stepped in with a student teacher.

"Boys and girls," Ms. Oshida announced. "Ms. Rizzoli will be in charge of the class for the next few minutes."

Then Ms. Oshida turned to Nancy. "Nancy Drew," she said. "May I see you in my office please?"

8

Back to Earth

This must be a bad dream, Nancy thought as she followed Ms. Oshida.

"Come in, Nancy," Ms. Oshida said, opening the door to her office.

Nancy wasn't surprised to see Ms. Zagon standing next to Ms. Oshida's desk.

Ms. Oshida sat down and picked up a copy of the *Carlton News*. She opened it and began to read:

"'According to Nancy Drew, Ms. Zagon means no harm. She just wants to take over planet Earth.'"

Nancy felt her face turn red.

"Can you explain this article, Nancy?" Ms. Oshida asked.

Nancy took a deep breath and explained everything to Ms. Oshida and Ms. Zagon.

"So you almost believed I was an alien?" Ms. Zagon asked.

Nancy nodded slowly. "I hope you're not mad, Ms. Zagon."

Ms. Zagon smiled and shook her head. "When I was your age, I imagined myself as a queen of another planet. I guess my wish finally came true."

"Does this mean your case is closed, Detective Drew?" Ms. Oshida asked Nancy.

"Almost," Nancy said. "I just need to ask Ms. Zagon a few questions. They're really important."

"Go ahead, Nancy," Ms. Zagon said.

"Why was there a picture of space aliens in your car?" Nancy asked.

Ms. Oshida peered over her glasses at Ms. Zagon. "Space aliens?"

"Oh, that!" Ms. Zagon laughed. "My friends and I dressed up as aliens last Halloween. I found the photo in the glove compartment."

Nancy smiled. Then she went on. "My next question is, why did Katie's parrot fly out of your house speaking so strange? It sounded something like . . . Veegatesgrossmudder?"

"Lester probably heard me talking on the telephone to my grandmother," Ms. Zagon explained. "Grandma speaks only German,"

German! Nancy thought. So it wasn't the secret language of Planet Zagon!

"*Wie gehtes dir, Grossmutter* means, 'How are you, Grandmother?' " Ms. Zagon said.

"Any more questions, Nancy?" Ms. Oshida asked.

"One more," Nancy said quickly. "Why did Peaches get so fat?"

Ms. Zagon looked confused. "Peaches?"

"I can answer that," Ms. Oshida said. "Mrs. Reynolds was supposed to announce this week that your hamster is about to have babies."

"Oh!" Nancy said.

Nancy returned to the classroom

with Ms. Zagon. She stood in front of the class and explained everything.

"So you're not an alien, Ms. Zagon?" Mike asked.

Ms. Zagon pointed to the top of her head. "See? No antennas."

"Too bad!" Jason groaned.

Orson Wong held up his copy of the *Carlton News*. "Then this newspaper is one big lie!" he shouted, ripping the paper in half.

"It is not!" Brenda cried. But it was too late. The rest of the class was ripping their newspapers in half, too.

Ms. Zagon clapped her hands for attention. "Okay, class. Now that we've returned to Earth, how about that surprise I was talking about?"

The class murmured excitedly.

"Where is it, Ms. Zagon?" Phoebe Archer asked.

"It's outside, behind the school," Ms. Zagon said. "Can anyone guess what it is?"

Nancy smiled to herself. Could it be the time capsule?

*   *   *

The class had fun digging up the time capsule and looking through it.

"It's like going back in time," Emily said, trying on a bead necklace.

"Ms. Zagon?" Nancy asked. "Do you think we could make our own time capsule when Mrs. Reynolds comes back?"

"That's a great idea, Nancy," Ms. Zagon said. The rest of the class agreed.

"What should we put in it?" Bess asked.

Ms. Zagon held up a copy of the *Carlton News*. "You could start with this."

Nancy laughed with the rest of the class. But she had a better idea. She would write her own composition for the time capsule. It would be called "Why I Love Mysteries."

That night Nancy sat on her bed. She opened her detective notebook to a clean page. Then she wrote:

One thing I learned during this "space case" is that rumors can

71

sometimes be exciting or funny, but you have to work to find out if they're true.

Nancy gazed out the window just in time to see another shooting star.

I'm glad Ms. Zagon is not an alien.

And I'm *very* glad I'm a detective!

Case closed.

THE
NANCY DREW
NOTEBOOKS®

Do you know a younger Nancy Drew fan?

Now there are mysteries just for them!

Nancy Drew and The Clue Crew®

Test your detective skills with more Clue Crew cases!

From Aladdin • Published by Simon & Schuster

Nancy Drew and The Clue Crew®

Test your detective skills with more Clue Crew cases!

Visit NancyDrew.com for the inside scoop!

From Aladdin · KIDS.SimonandSchuster.com